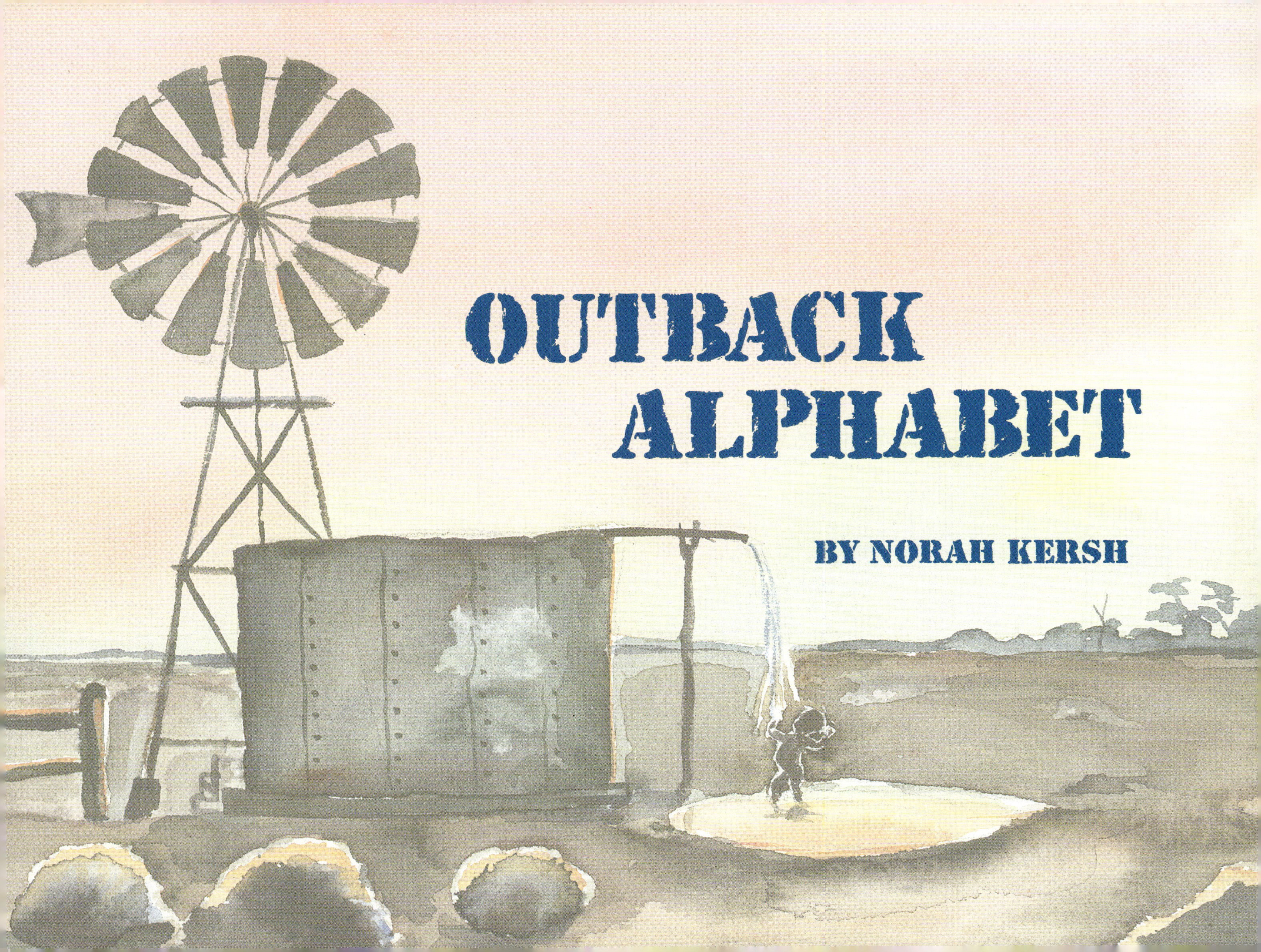

OUTBACK ALPHABET

BY NORAH KERSH

First Printed 1999

Reprinted 1999, 2001, 2004, 2007, 2009

National Library of Australia Cataloguing-in-Publication entry:

Author:	Kersh, Norah
Title:	Outback Alphabet
ISBN:	978 0 86439 211 4 (pbk.) 978 1921555 15 2 (hardback.)
Subjects:	I. Alphabet rhymes. I. Title.
Dewey Number:	398.8

Typeset in Times 24 pt.

Published by Boolarong Press, Salisbury, Brisbane, Australia.

Printed and bound by Watson Ferguson & Company, Salisbury, Brisbane, Australia.

To Tyler John

whose three years gave us much joy

Acknowledgments

I would like to thank all those whose help has made this book possible, especially all school of distance educators for their unfailing encouragement to our children; in particular my warm gratitude to Karen Redman, from Mount Isa School of the Air, for her kind and constructive advice in the preparation of this book.

Marie Mahood, my friend and neighbour from remote outback, who encouraged me all the way; and my family for their love and constant support in a doubtless biased opinion of my paintings.

Without the "wondrous glory" of the outback itself and the stalwart neighbours and friends who people it, I would not have the inspiration to do their sketches of life.

Other books illustrated by the author:

"Outback Countout" Norah Kersh

"Through Deep Waters" Fran Spora

"Reflections from the Desert" Pat Cullen

A is for Ant.
Ally digs in the hot red sand
As ants go scurrying overland.

B is for Baby.
Baby on a blanket blue
Saw the bird as down it flew.

C is for Cat.

Cat on a cubby sleeps in the sun
I mix mudcakes having fun.

D is for Dad.
Dad is home, he's my best mate
On his old horse, life is great.

E is for Eggs.
Eggs are hiding in the grass
Emu watches as we pass.

F is for Fun.

Fun dressing up from this big box,
In frills and flounces on old frocks.

G is for Gate.
Gates can be the best fun,
Kate can balance on this one.

H is for Hat.
Hats on heads in the sun all day,
Making shade for work or play.

I is for Insect.
Insects flitting here and there,
Insects buzzing everywhere.

J is for Jug.
Jug of milk and jam I see,
Is it time for morning tea?

K is for Kick.
Kick to show who's boss today
Watch me as I hop away.

Take a bandage, here we go.

Mission accomplished, if the chair holds tight!

W is for Windmill.
Windmills going round and round
Pumping water from underground.

X is for X-ray.
X-ray shows the bone I broke
Using crutches is no joke.

Y is for Yellow.
Yellow sunflowers tall and bright
Love the sun but not the night.

Z is for Zig-zag.
Zig-zag riding up the hill,
Hope he doesn't have a spill.

OUTBACK ALPHABET

Tyler John Kersh, Sean's and Katrina's beloved son, was a typical Queensland boy from the bush.

He put so much into his short life, and brought delight to so many.

His tragic death brought grief beyond description. Yet even after his death,

through the donation of his organs, other children were given the opportunity to carry on their lives.

Tyler has joined the ranks of the heroes of history, who through death, gave the gift of life to others.

Norah Kersh

Other books by
Norah Kersh

- Outback Countout
- Outback Songs
- Grandma's Precious Chest
- Outback Doctor
- *Coming soon*: Outback School

COMET